W9-AYH-513

Hans Christian Andersen
Lisbeth Zwerger

THE NIGHTINGALE

Translated from the Danish by Anthea Bell

A MICHAEL NEUGEBAUER BOOK
NORTH-SOUTH BOOKS / NEW YORK / LONDON

In China, as of course you know, the Emperor is Chinese, and so are all his people. This story happened many years ago, but that makes it all the more worth hearing. Old tales should be told again before they are forgotten.

The Emperor had the most magnificent palace in the world, made all of fine porcelain, so expensive and so fragile and delicate that you hardly dared touch it. Out in the garden grew wonderfully beautiful flowers, and the loveliest of all had little silver bells tied to them that rang as you went by, so that you couldn't fail to notice them. Everything in the Emperor's garden was so ingeniously laid out, and the garden itself stretched so far, that even the gardener didn't know where it ended. If you went on beyond it you came to a very beautiful wood, with tall trees and deep lakes. This wood went all the way down to the deep blue sea. Great ships could sail right in under its branches, and in the branches there lived a nightingale who sang so sweetly that even the poor fisherman, busy as he was when he came down to the sea at night to cast his nets, would stop and listen to its song. "Dear God, how beautiful it is!" he said. Then he had to get down to his work, and he forgot the bird, but when he came out the next night and the nightingale sang again, he said the same: "Dear God, how beautiful it is!"

Travelers from every country in the world visited the Emperor's city, and marvelled at the city itself and the palace and the garden, but when they heard the nightingale every one of them said, "Ah, that's the best thing of all!"

And when the travelers were home they said what they had seen, and learned men wrote books about the city and the palace and the garden, not forgetting the nightingale: they praised that most of all. And poets wrote wonderful verses about the nightingale who lived in the wood by the deep sea.

The books went all over the world, and at last they came to the Emperor too.

He sat and read and read, nodding his head again and again with pleasure, for he was delighted with the wonderful descriptions of his city and his palace and his garden. And then he read: "But the nightingale is best of all."

"What's all this?" said the Emperor. "Nightingale? I never heard of it. So there is such a bird in my Imperial realm, in my own garden, and I haven't heard it? Well, to think what one may learn from books!"

And he summoned his Lord in Waiting, so very grand a gentleman that if anyone of lesser rank so much as spoke to him or asked him a question he simply said, "P!" which means nothing at all.

"They say there is a remarkable bird called the nightingale here," said the Emperor, "and they say it's the finest thing in all my Empire. Why has nobody ever told me about this bird?"

"I never heard of it myself," said the Lord in Waiting. "It's never been presented at Court."

"I want it to come and sing for me this evening," said the Emperor. "It seems all the world knows what I have here, except me!"

"I never heard of it myself," repeated the Lord in Waiting. "But I'll look for it, and I'll find it."

Where was it to be found, though? The Lord in Waiting ran up and down all the flights of stairs, through great halls, down corridors, and no one he met had ever heard tell of the nightingale. So the Lord in Waiting went back to the Emperor and said it must be just a story made up by the people who wrote the books.

"Your Imperial Majesty mustn't believe everything he reads in books; they are full of invention and not to be trusted."

"But the book in which I read it," said the Emperor, "was sent to me by the high and mighty Emperor of Japan, so it must be true. I want to hear the nightingale! It is to come here this evening, and if it doesn't I'll have the whole Court thumped in the stomach, right after they've had their supper."

"Tsing-pe!" said the Lord in Waiting, and he went off again and ran up and down the flights of stairs, through the halls and down the corridors, and half the Court went with him, not wanting to be thumped in the stomach. They all asked about the remarkable nightingale, known to everyone else in the world but not to the Court. At last they found a poor little girl in the kitchen, who said, "The nightingale? Oh, yes. I know the nightingale very well, and oh, how it can sing! I'm allowed to take some of the food left over from the table to my poor sick mother in the evenings, and she lives down by the shore, so when I'm on my way back I stop for a rest in the wood and I hear the nightingale sing. It brings tears to my eyes, as if my mother were kissing me."

"Little kitchenmaid," said the Lord in Waiting, "I will get you a steady job here in the kitchen and permission to watch the Emperor eat his dinner if you can take us to the nightingale, for it is summoned to Court this evening."

So half the Court went out to the wood where the nightingale sang. And as they were going along a cow began to moo.

"We've found the nightingale!" said the courtiers. "What a powerful voice for such a little creature! I've heard it somewhere before."

"No, those are cows," said the little kitchenmaid. "We aren't nearly there yet."

Then they heard the frogs croaking in the pond.

"Exquisite!" said the Imperial Palace Chaplain. "Now that I hear it, its song is like little church bells."

"No, those are frogs," said the little kitchenmaid. "But I think we'll soon hear the nightingale now."

And then the nightingale began to sing.

"There it is!" said the little girl. "Listen, listen! It is sitting up there." And she pointed to a small grey bird up in the branches of the trees.

"Can it be true?" said the Lord in Waiting. "I'd never have thought it! It looks such an ordinary bird. All its bright plumage must have fallen away at the sight of such grand people!"

"Little nightingale," called the kitchenmaid, "our gracious Emperor wants you to sing for him."

"He's very welcome," said the nightingale, and it sang so beautifully, it was a joy to hear that song.

"Like glass bells!" said the Lord in Waiting. "And see the way its little throat quivers! And to think we never heard it before—what a success it will be at Court!"

"Shall I sing for the Emperor again?" asked the nightingale, who thought the Emperor himself was present.

"My dear, good little nightingale," said the Lord in Waiting. "I am pleased and proud to invite you to a party at Court this evening, where you will delight his Imperial Majesty with your lovely song."

"It sounds best out here in the green wood," said the nightingale, but it went along with them willingly enough, on hearing it was the Emperor's wish.

What a cleaning and a polishing there was at the palace! The walls and floors, all made of porcelain, shone in the light of thousands of golden lamps. The loveliest of flowers, the chiming ones from the Emperor's garden, were placed along the corridor. With all the hurry and bustle, there was such a draft that it made the bells ring out, and you couldn't hear yourself speak.

In the middle of the great hall where the Emperor sat they placed a golden perch for the nightingale. The little girl, who now had the official title of Kitchenmaid, was allowed to stand behind the door. The entire Court was there, all dressed in their best, and they were all gazing at the little grey bird. The Emperor nodded to it.

And the nightingale sang so sweetly that tears rose to the Emperor's eyes and flowed down his cheeks, and then the nightingale sang yet more beautifully, so that its song went right to the heart. The Emperor was so delighted that he said the nightingale was to have the Emperor's own golden slipper to wear around its neck. But the nightingale thanked him and said it already had its reward.

"I have seen tears in the eyes of the Emperor, and what more could I wish for? An Emperor's tears have wonderful power; God knows that's reward enough for me." And it sang again in its sweet, lovely voice.

"That's the prettiest thing I ever heard," said the ladies standing by, and they poured water into their mouths and tried to trill when they were spoken to, thinking they would be nightingales too. Even the lackeys and the chambermaids expressed satisfaction, which is saying a good deal, for such folk are the very hardest to please. In short, the nightingale was a great success.

And now it was to stay at Court, and have its own cage, and be allowed out twice by day and once by night. Twelve menservants were to go with it, each holding tight to a silken ribbon tied to the bird's leg. Of course, going out like that was no pleasure at all. The whole city was talking of the marvelous bird, and if two friends met, one would say, "Night," and the other, "Gale," and they sighed, and each knew exactly what the other meant. Eleven grocers' children were named after the bird, but not one of them could sing a note.

One day a big parcel came for the Emperor, with *Nightingale* written on it.
"Here's a new book about our famous bird," said the Emperor. But it wasn't a book,
it was a little mechanical toy in a box, an artificial nightingale. It was meant to
look like the real one, but it was covered all over with diamonds and rubies and
sapphires. As soon as you wound the bird up it sang one of the real nightingale's
songs, and its tail went up and down, all shining with silver and gold. It had a
little ribbon around its neck with the words: "The Emperor of Japan's nightingale
is a poor thing beside the nightingale of the Emperor of China."
"How exquisite!" everyone said, and they gave the man who had brought the
artificial bird the title of Lord High Nightingale Bringer.
"Now they can sing together. We'll have a duet," said the Court.
So sing together they did, but it wasn't quite right, for the real nightingale sang in
its own way, and the artificial bird's song worked by means of a cylinder inside it.
"It's not the new bird's fault," said the Emperor's Master of the Music. "It keeps perfect
time, and performs in my very own style." So the artificial bird was to sing alone.
It was just as great a success as the real bird, and then it was so much prettier to
look at! It glittered like jewelry.
It sang the same song thirty-three times, and still it wasn't tired. The Court would
happily have heard the song again, but the Emperor thought it was time for the real
nightingale to sing. But where had it gone? No one had noticed it flying out of the
open window, out and away, back to its own green wood.

"What's all this?" said the Emperor, and all the courtiers said the nightingale was a most ungrateful creature. "But we still have the better bird," they said, and the mechanical nightingale had to sing the same song again, for the thirty-fourth time. It was a difficult song, and the Court didn't quite know it by heart yet. The Master of the Music praised the bird to the skies, and actually stated that it was better than the real nightingale, not just because of its plumage, glittering with so many lovely diamonds, but inside too.

"For you see, my lords, and particularly your Imperial Majesty, you can never tell just what the real bird is going to sing, but with the artificial bird it's all settled. It will sing like this and it won't sing any other way. You can understand it, you can open it up and see how human minds made it, where the wheels and cylinders lie, how they work and how they all go around."

"My own opinion entirely," said everyone, and the Master of the Music got permission to show the bird to all the people the next Sunday, for the Emperor said they should hear it too. And hear it they did, and they were as happy as if they had gotten tipsy on tea, for tea is what the Chinese drink; and they all said "Ooh!" and pointed their fingers in the air, and nodded. However, the poor fisherman who used to listen to the real nightingale said, "It sounds nice enough, and quite like the real bird, but there's something missing, I don't know what."

And the real nightingale was banished from the Emperor's domains.

The artificial bird had a place on a silk cushion next to the Emperor's bed. All the presents of gold and jewels it had been given lay around it, and it bore the title of Imperial Bedside Singer in Chief, so it took first place on the left side: the Emperor thought the side upon which the heart lies was the better one, and even an Emperor's heart is on his left. And the Master of the Music wrote a book, in twenty-five volumes, about the mechanical bird. The book was very long and very learned, and full of hard words in Chinese, so all the people at Court pretended to have read it, for fear of looking stupid and being thumped in the stomach.

So it went on for a year. The Emperor, the Court, and all the other Chinese now knew every little trill of the mechanical bird's song by heart, but they liked it all the better for that. They could join in the song themselves, and they did too. Even the street urchins sang, "Tweet-tweet-tweet, cluck-cluck-cluck-cluck!" and the Emperor sang, too. How delightful it all was!

One evening, however, as the artificial bird was singing its very best, and the Emperor lay in his bed listening, it went, "Twang!" and something broke inside it. The wheels whirred around and the music stopped.

The Emperor jumped straight out of bed, and summoned his own doctor, but there was nothing the doctor could do. So they fetched the watchmaker, and after much talk and much tinkering about with it, he got the bird to work again after a fashion. However, he said it mustn't be made to sing very often, because the little pegs on the cylinders had worn out and there was no way of replacing them without spoiling the tune. This was very sad indeed. They let the mechanical bird sing just once a year, and even that was a strain on it, but the Master of the Music used to make a little speech crammed with difficult words, saying the bird was still as good as ever, and so then of course it was, just as he said.

Five years passed by, and then the whole country was in great distress, for the people all loved their Emperor, and now he was sick and likely to die. A new Emperor had already been chosen, and people stood in the street and asked the Lord in Waiting how the old one was.

He only said, "P!" and shook his head.

The Emperor lay in his great, magnificent bed, and he was cold and pale. The whole Court thought he was dead already, and the courtiers went off to pay their respects to the new Emperor. The lackeys of the bedchamber got together for a gossip, and the maids in waiting were having a big coffee party. Cloth was laid down in all the halls and corridors, so that you could hear no footfall, and all was quiet, very quiet. But the Emperor was not dead yet. Stiff and pale, he lay in his bed of state, which was hung with velvet and with heavy golden tassels. There was a window open up above, and moonlight shone in on the Emperor and the mechanical nightingale.

The poor Emperor could hardly draw breath, and he felt as if something were sitting on his chest. He opened his eyes, and saw that it was Death sitting there. Death was wearing the Emperor's golden crown, and he had the Emperor's Imperial golden sabre in one hand and his magnificent banner in the other. And strange faces peered out from among the folds of the great velvet hangings of the bed: some were grim and hideous, others blessed and mild. They were the Emperor's good deeds and bad deeds all looking at him as Death sat there on his heart.

"Remember this?" they whispered, one by one. "Remember that?" And they reminded him of so many things that the sweat broke out on his forehead.

"No, no! I never knew!" said the Emperor. "Music!" he cried. "Music on the great Chinese drum, to keep me from hearing what you say!"

But on they went, and Death kept nodding like a Chinese mandarin at everything they said.

"Music, music!" cried the Emperor. "Sing, my little golden bird, oh, sing! I have given you gold and treasure, I myself hung my golden slipper around your neck, so sing for me now, sing!"

But the bird was silent, for there wasn't anyone there to wind it up, and it could not sing without being wound. And Death gazed and gazed at the Emperor through his great empty eye sockets, and all was still, all was terribly still.

And at that moment the loveliest of songs was heard coming in through the window. It was the real nightingale sitting in the branches outside. It had heard of the Emperor's sickness, and so it had come to sing him a song of hope and comfort. And as it sang, the phantom shapes faded away, the blood flowed faster and faster through the Emperor's weak limbs, and Death himself listened and said, "Go on, go on, little nightingale!"

"Yes, if you give me that fine gold sabre! Yes, if you give me that gorgeous banner! Yes, if you will give me the Emperor's crown!" So Death gave all those treasures up, each for one of the nightingale's songs, and the nightingale sang on and on. It sang of the quiet churchyard where white roses grow and the air is fragrant with elder flowers, and the fresh grass is wet with the tears of the bereaved. Then Death longed for his own garden again, and he drifted away out of the window like cold white mist.

"Thank you, thank you," said the Emperor. "Most blessed of little birds, I know you now! I drove you away from my domains, yet you have sung away all those evil visions from my bed, and driven Death from my heart. How can I reward you?"

"You have rewarded me already," said the nightingale. "I brought tears to your eyes the first time I sang to you, and I will never forget those tears. They are the jewels that rejoice a singer's heart. But you must sleep now, and be fresh and strong when you wake. Now I will sing for you."

The nightingale sang, and the Emperor fell asleep into a sweet, gentle, and refreshing slumber.

The sun was shining in on him through the window when he woke, feeling strong and healthy. None of his servants was back, for they all thought he was dead, but the nightingale still sat there singing.

"You must stay with me forever," said the Emperor. "You need never sing unless you want to, and I will break the artificial bird into a thousand pieces."

"Don't do that," said the nightingale. "It did the best it could, after all, so you should keep it. I cannot live or nest in a palace; but let me come to you when I feel like it, and I'll sit on the branch outside your window and sing in the evening, to gladden your heart and fill it with thoughts. I will sing of those who are happy and those who are sad, I will sing of the bad and the good around you. A little singing bird flies far and wide, to the poor fisherman and the peasant's hut, to people very far from you and your Court. I love your heart more than I love your crown, yet that crown seems to have something sacred about it. I will come and sing for you, but you must promise me one thing."

"Anything," said the Emperor, and he stood there in the imperial robes he had put on again, holding his heavy golden sabre to his breast.

"All I ask is that you will not let anyone know you have a little bird who tells you everything; that will be best."

Then the nightingale flew away.

The Emperor's servants came in to look at him lying dead, and they stood there amazed.

"Good morning," said the Emperor.

First North-South Books edition published in 1999
Copyright © 1984 by Nord-Süd Verlag AG, Gossau Zürich, Switzerland
First published in German under the title Die Nachtigall
English translation copyright © 1984 by Nord-Süd Verlag AG, Gossau Zürich, Switzerland

All rights reserved.
No part of this book may be reproduced or utilized in any form
or by any means, electronic or mechanical, including photocopying,
recording, or any information storage and retrieval system,
without permission in writing from the publisher.

Distributed in the United States by North-South Books Inc., New York.

Library of Congress Cataloging-in-Publication Data is available.
A CIP catalogue record for this book is available from The British Library.

ISBN 0-7358-1118-0 (trade binding) 10 9 8 7 6 5 4 3 2 1
ISBN 0-7358-1120-2 (paperback) 10 9 8 7 6 5 4 3 2 1

Printed in Italy

For more information about our books, and the authors and artists who create them,
visit our web site: http://www.northsouth.com

The following titles illustrated by Lisbeth Zwerger are
available from NORTH-SOUTH BOOKS:
LITTLE RED CAP · Jacob and Wilhelm Grimm
THE SWINEHERD · Hans Christian Andersen
LULLABIES, LYRICS AND GALLOWS SONGS · Christian Morgenstern
DWARF NOSE · Wilhelm Hauff
LITTLE HOBBIN · Theodor Storm
THE LEGEND OF ROSEPETAL · Clemens Brentano
THE WIZARD OF OZ · L. Frank Baum
THE DELIVERERS OF THEIR COUNTRY · E. Nesbit
THE CANTERVILLE GHOST · Oscar Wilde
THE ART OF LISBETH ZWERGER
NOAH'S ARK retold by Heinz Janisch